Meet My Grandparents

Papa Lemon was born in West, Mississippi on Dec. 6, 1896, and passed away on Oct. 29, 1973. The last time I saw my grandfather was when they closed the coffin at his funeral. I could not believe that would be the

Mama Sarah and Papa Lemon

end. No more games of checkers or taking me to Miss Annie B's General Store for candy or pop. Nine years of knowing him was not enough, but I thank God for giving me the vision to share my grandfather with the world. Kids of all ages, I give you my grandfather, Papa Lemon.

Mama Sarah, the wife of Papa Lemon, was born in West, Mississippi on Jan. 26, 1903. My grandmother lived to be 101 years old. She was the sweetest lady I ever knew. I never heard my grandmother raise her voice. I loved for her to tell me stories about how she grew up, and the life she had with Papa Lemon. She found good in everyone, never seeing the negative in people. With her last words she looked to Heaven and said "It's so beautiful," and passed away, and that's how she was so beautiful.

Papa Lemon and Mama Sarah had nine children and numerous grand and great grand children.

D0709045

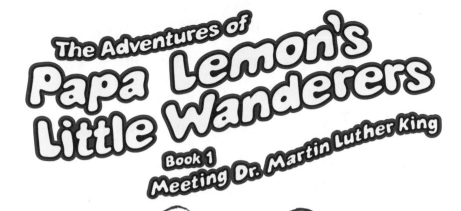

The Adventures of Papa Lemon's Little Wanderers

Book 1
Meeting Dr. Martin Luther King

written by Lehman Riley
edited by Megan Austin
illustrated by Joshua Wallace
www.papalemonedu.com

Nikki, The Leader

Carlos, The Protector

Baby Buck, The Know-It-All

AJ, The Worrier

Kaya, The Diva

Papa Lemon and Mama Sarah, The Neighborhood Grandparents

It was the first week of classes at Lincoln Elementary School in a small town in Mississippi. The fifth grade teacher, Miss Kim, was finishing her lessons as most of the fifteen kids in her class watched the clock intently. It was almost time for the bell to ring—the start of the weekend!

As the last couple of minutes ticked away, the kids already had their minds on their weekend plans. BRRIIIING!!! The school bell sounded and the children darted from their seats toward the door. Before any of them

could step into the hall, they heard Miss Kim calling for attention.

"Hold it! I have some homework for you," said Miss Kim.

The kids shuffled back to their seats, groaning about the work that would interrupt their weekend.

"Our history lesson shouldn't end here,

kids. To continue this lesson, I want each of you to research an American leader from history. You may choose one of the leaders we have pictured in the classroom, or choose one of your own. When you come back Monday, be prepared to share your discoveries with the class."

The impatient children immediately started searching the room for ideas, their eyes resting on the wall where Miss Kim had arranged a collage of great Americans. The classroom began to buzz with chatter between friends as the kids decided which leader to choose for the report.

An adventurous group of friends gathered near the collage and searched for an exciting leader they could learn about over the weekend. As other kids made their choices and began to leave the classroom, the friends found that they weren't satisfied with the selections on the wall.

"Our history book says a little bit about each of these people but I'm tired of those same

old stories. I don't know who to pick," said
Baby Buck, the shortest but most outspoken
member of the group of longtime friends. "Hey,
Nikki, what do you think?"

Nikki heard Baby Buck but didn't answer
him. She was thinking about her own project
and which great American leader she would
choose to share with the class. Nikki enjoyed
history, and just about every other subject in
school. She had already decided she would

do some research on the computer over the
weekend and would be proud to give her report
on Monday, though she wasn't sure which
leader she would choose.

On the walk home from school Baby
Buck, Nikki, Carlos, Kaya and AJ talked about
the assignment, discussing and complaining,
complaining and discussing. The kids took
their usual route, passing Miss Annie B's

General Store and stopping at Papa Lemon and
Mama Sarah's house for their afternoon snacks.
Papa Lemon and Mama Sarah lived on a huge
farm, complete with a watermelon patch, plum
trees, blueberries, grapes and peanuts. They
also had cows, pigs, chickens and horses. As
the Grandfather of the neighborhood, Papa
Lemon knew each of the kids and their parents
by name and was always happy to talk to them.

The kids were complaining about their assignment between mouthfuls of fruit while Papa Lemon picked blueberries for Mama Sarah's jam.

"Sounds like you have some kind of problem, kids," said Papa Lemon.

Kaya answered, "Yes, Sir. Miss Kim wants us to write about a great leader in our history…"

"But we're tired of the same old stories. There has to be more to history than what our text book tells us," interrupted Baby Buck.

All of the kids nodded in agreement, "and before Kaya could explain further, everyone began to voice their opinions about the assignment.

"Hold it! Hold it! One at a time, kids, one at a time!" Papa Lemon instructed the clamoring group.

"Yeah! Quiet down," shouted Nikki.

The kids hushed and settled down around Papa Lemon on the front porch as Nikki continued. "Grandfather, did you ever have a

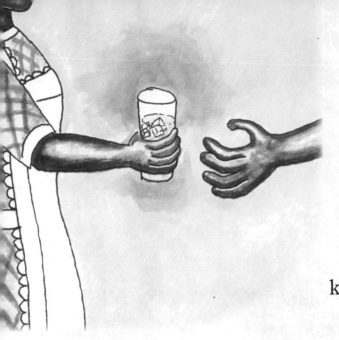

problem like this when you were a kid?"

"Sure I did," replied Papa Lemon, "and just like you, I didn't know what to do."

AJ said, "Papa Lemon, you know so much about so many people in history. If you had the same problem as us, how did you learn about so many of our ancestors?"

Mama Sarah handed Papa Lemon a glass of lemonade. "Don't you think it's time to tell them about the train?" she said quietly.

"Yes," he said with a sparkle in his eyes. "Let me tell you a story," said Papa Lemon.

"About what?" Nikki asked.

"My train."

"Your train? What train? We've never seen you with a train!" the kids shouted.

"Hold on, hold on. Let me show you.

Come, follow me to the shed where I keep it."

When they got inside the shed, Papa
Lemon told Carlos and AJ to pull off the big
sheet that covered the train. As the sheet fell
away, the kids could not believe how beautiful
the train was! It was bright red with gold trim
and gold gears. It was much bigger than they
had imagined it. Papa Lemon only had the

engine but it had enough room inside for at least five kids.

Carlos asked, "How can this train help us with history?"

"You kids sit down and let me tell you a story about how this train helped me with history.

"I can remember being about seven years old and riding down

the tracks with my father in this very same train. What a great feeling that was—watching him pull the switches and blow the whistle, smelling the smoke as it came out of the stack! To me there was nothing better."

"What about school? Didn't you go?" Kaya interrupted.

"Yes, I did. That was the only way I was allowed to ride. I had to do my school lessons first. Then my father would let me ride with him."

"Wasn't it hard to get all your school work done in time?" Carlos asked.

Papa Lemon answered, "Yes, but I wanted to be on the train so I did what I had to do to be able to ride with my father.

"Now, a few years went by and I wanted to make my father proud of me, so I got a job at the train yard. I made sure I was always on time for work and I worked hard. I kept this train sparkling, but parts were always breaking. The time came when the train was getting too expensive to run. My boss told me it was time

14

to replace it. They were going to take it to the junkyard. Without hesitation, I asked if I could buy it. My boss looked at me as if I was crazy and asked, 'Why do you want this old train?' I told him I just couldn't bear to see the train rust out in a junkyard. He said that I could have the train for free since I felt that strongly about it.

"When I heard that I could keep the train, I jumped up and gave him the biggest hug. After he got his wind back, he called the crane

operator
to lift the
train onto
a huge
truck.
The truck
slowly
made its
way to my
house. For the
next two months,
I built this shed around
the train. After I finished the shed, I started
cleaning my train. It took weeks of polishing,
oiling and painting. When I was done, it looked
like new.

"History was the one thing I loved as
much as the train. I always wondered what it
would be like to go back to the good old days. I

thought maybe I could make my train go back in time, so I pulled wires out and added some connectors and tubes and screwed in two dials. The left dial was to bring people back in time and the right dial was to bring people back to the present day. This train is the answer to all of your history questions. This train will take you to whatever period in history you want to go to."

"How?" the kids shouted with puzzled looks.

"Well, it started sixty years ago with a glass of lemonade that fell into the control panel. Now, this was not your ordinary lemonade. This was my father's special blend. You see, when I was a kid, I used to hear my father and mother laughing with their friends, talking about how good the lemonade was. They all said it reminded them of the old days. The taste would take them back to their childhood, when they would play kick-the-can or hide-and-seek in the cornfield. They used to ask my father how he made his lemonade.

My father would laugh and tell them it was a secret family recipe and that's how it was going to stay. 'There's plenty more in the cellar,' he would say. Twenty years later, my father gave me the recipe, and Sarah made sure we always had an ice-cold pitcher in the icebox.

"One evening I had just finished wiring the control panel and I wanted to see if I could make the engine idle. I pushed the ignition button and pulled the gearshift, but all I got was a little shake. Sarah came in with some lemonade and asked how everything was going. As she handed me the lemonade, the glass slipped out of my hand and fell into the control panel. I was sure I had wrecked everything.

"Sarah took off her apron and started wiping up what she could. We looked at each other, but I couldn't speak. Sarah said, 'Give it another try. What's the worst that could happen?' I took a deep breath and pulled the gearshift back.

"To my surprise there was no shaking. The engine was running smoothly! Suddenly, sparks started coming from the panel. The next thing I knew, I was gone.

"I found myself on a grassy hill looking at something I could not believe. My father and mother were young. They were walking down a dirt road right in front of me, but they didn't even see me. I knew at that moment that the lemonade had transported me back in time. It worked! The lemonade was the magic that made the train go back in time. I just hoped it would do the same to bring me home. I set the dial for 1939 and turned the switch to the right. The train started to rumble and off I went. In an instant, I was back in the shed.

"You kids should have seen Sarah's face! I thought she was going to faint and I don't blame her. She yelled, 'What happened? Where did you go?' I told her what had happened and what I had seen.

"I kept all my trips through history a secret for years. I would set the dial for all

different times in history. It was fun to watch
everything. Now I am too old to go on the trips.
Now it's your turn to go and learn about our
great past. It is your turn to experience the big
events and the events you have never heard of.

"When you go back in time, don't try and
change anything, only watch. You can talk to
people but don't let them know you are from
the future. Blend in."

"How can we blend in if our clothes don't

look like theirs?" Kaya asked.

Papa Lemon answered, "When I took my trips, I found clothes from each time period I visited and brought them to Sarah to make copies. There is a trunk full of them in the attic. Have Sarah take you up there and pick out whatever you need for the trip you want to take."

Then Papa Lemon pulled out a big, dusty book. "Here is a book of all my travels. Look through it and decide on a time to visit."

The kids ran through the house and

found Mama Sarah in the kitchen making
cookies. They were full of excitement, tugging
on her apron, asking about the trunk that
was in the attic. They begged her to take
them to the attic to find some clothes for their
adventures. The kids dragged Mama Sarah up
to the attic where they found the dusty trunk in
the corner.

The kids sat around the big trunk,
looking through the book of Papa Lemon's
travels. "Let's go back and see the cowboys
of the Wild West! YEEEEHAAA!" shouted

Baby Buck.

"I want to go back to see the slave times," piped Carlos.

"Hey, that's not fair!" whined Kaya, who was the oldest and most opinionated of the group. "We don't want to do just boy things! I want to go back in time and see some ballet dancers."

Nikki interrupted the bickering. "Let's not go back too far in time on our first adventure. We don't know what's going to happen or what to expect." The kids looked at each other and decided Nikki was right. They would have to agree on something that was not too far in the past for their first adventure.

"Where will we go?" wondered Carlos as the kids looked through the old clothes. It was a good question. All of the kids had ideas about what they wanted to see and who they wanted to meet on their journey back in time.

"I know!" Nikki answered. "Let's go back to a time that we always hear about; let's go to hear Martin Luther King give the speech

that rocked the world—'I Have A Dream'.
We'll go back to that day and listen to what Dr.
King said. Most of all, we'll watch the people's
reactions. When we come back, we can tell
Miss Kim what we learned about the speech."

The kids ran down the stairs dressed
in 1960's clothing, excited for Papa Lemon to
see them. Papa Lemon greeted them at the

back door with a laugh. "There are my Little Wanderers!"

"Hey! The Little Wanderers! That's a great name for a group of kids that travels through time!" interrupted AJ. "That's what we should call ourselves!" The other kids nodded in agreement.

"You look like you're ready to go. Now, let's go over the instructions on how to use the train," Papa Lemon said.

They all went out to the shed and climbed into the train. The wide-eyed kids gathered around the control panel so Papa Lemon could show them how to operate the train. Papa Lemon demonstrated how to set the destination date with the left dial and the current date with the right dial. "Don't forget to switch the lever to the left when you go back in time and to the right when you want to come home," instructed Papa Lemon. "Are you kids ready for your adventures?"

They all shouted, "Yes!"

Carlos stepped to the front of the engine

as Papa Lemon climbed down. "You kids be careful," he said as he waved them on.

As Nikki set the dial to 1963, AJ started to object to the trip, worried that it might be a bad idea. Just as AJ opened his mouth, Carlos switched the lever to the left and pulled

the gearshift. Off they went! Kaya and AJ held each other with their eyes closed and their mouths open, Nikki laughed with Baby Buck and Carlos watched out the window.

The Little Wanderers stepped out of the train and looked at each other. They were standing in an old train yard. They could see the Washington monument rising tall and proud over a large group of people several blocks away. They were amazed by the size of the crowd! Curiosity propelled the kids toward the large mass of people.

"Follow me, I know where to go," said Baby Buck as he darted toward the front of the crowd.

"Not so fast! I can't keep up!"

28

AJ called after him. Baby Buck heard him but his excitement carried him faster and farther into the gathering. As the Little Wanderers wormed their way to the front, they noticed that the voice they heard was getting louder and louder. Nikki looked between two men standing at the front of the assembly. "Look, there's Martin Luther King!" she shouted.

Dr. King was standing behind a podium on the stage. "When we let freedom ring, when we let it ring from every village and every hamlet, from every state and every city, we will be able to speed up to the day when all God's children, black men and white men, Jews and

Gentiles, Protestants and Catholics, will be able to join hands and sing the words of the old Negro spiritual. Free at last! Free at last! Thank God Almighty, we are free at last." With these last words,

Dr. King left the podium. The kids looked at each other. "We're too late! We missed his speech!" Baby Buck declared.

"No way!" shouted Carlos. "We did not come this far just to hear the end of his speech. Come on, you guys!"

"Not so fast! Where are you going?" Kaya called as Carlos led the group through the crowd and toward the back of the stage. Carlos

turned to answer her and crashed right into Dr.
King, falling at his feet.

Martin Luther King looked down at the
boy and smiled as he helped him up. "What's
the hurry? Are you okay?" he asked Carlos.

Kaya and Nikki nervously hid behind AJ,
unsure of what to say. "We told him not to go so
fast," Nikki said quietly.

Baby Buck explained that they missed

his speech and they wanted to meet him. "How does it feel to be a leader?" he asked. "It must be scary."

Dr. King laughed. "Yes," he said, "sometimes it's very frightening, but I think of the good things that will happen if I keep up the marches, the church meetings and if people keep meeting with the president to tell him how unfair things are. I have a lot of good friends like you and that makes being a leader easier."

Martin Luther King put his arms around the Little Wanderers. "I just have to keep the faith. I'm working hard so everyone can have equal rights. I would love to see the adults do what you kids are doing—walking and playing together with different races coming together, respecting each other, learning about each others' cultures. That is why I chose to be a leader, so that all races can be friends. As you kids know, we are going through hard times now. I'm working hard for the day when we can all be together and have houses in the same neighborhoods. America is a great country and I want it to be great for everyone.

"Kids, I have to go now, but I want you to remember this: treat people the way you would like to be treated. That is called the Golden Rule."

With those words, Dr. King walked away. The Little Wanderers looked at each other, amazed that they had talked to Martin Luther King.

Nikki was the first one to speak. "I can't

wait to tell Papa Lemon that we actually talked to Martin Luther King! Let's go home and tell him what we learned today!"

"We've been gone a long time. I bet my mom is looking all over for me. Besides, I'm hungry," AJ said. The kids agreed that it was time to go home. Carlos reminded everyone that they had to stay together. Since Baby Buck knew which way they had come, he led the troop back to the spot where they first came through.

They all piled into the train, holding onto the rails. Carlos was back at the switch. Baby Buck yelled out, "Why do you get to turn the switch? You did it last time! I want to do it!"

Kaya told Baby Buck it wasn't a big deal. "You can do it another time. Let's just get home," she said.

"Lets go! I told you, I'm hungry!" AJ whined and Carlos turned the switch and pulled the gearshift. In a split second, they were all back home.

"Wow! Let's find Grandfather!" Baby

Buck shouted, as they all ran into the house,
screaming excitedly. Papa Lemon looked up,
startled by the noise. "Welcome back," he said.
"Did you see anything?"

"Did we see anything? Boy, did we ever!

We saw Dr. Martin Luther King, except we didn't get to hear his whole speech," Kaya explained. The kids sat down around Papa Lemon's favorite chair and began to tell him what they saw.

"Dr. King told us that we should try to work things out and live together like brothers and sisters, not enemies," Carlos said.

"You're right. You kids need to remember what you saw and learned today. Try to treat others, regardless of what color skin, the same way you would want to be treated. This is called The Golden Rule," Papa Lemon explained.

After the kids left Papa Lemon's house, they read the entire speech and entered it into their journal just as Papa Lemon had instructed them to.

The following Monday in school, the Little Wanderers read their reports. "How did you learn so much about Dr. King's speech just over the weekend?" Miss Kim asked as they finished.

"Miss Kim, we all got together and

pretended we were there that day. It was so real that it was just like we took part. Isn't that right gang? It's just like we were there." Nikki said with a wink.

I hope you enjoyed this
adventure! Now how about a little
adventure of your own? Go to your
parents and ask them to tell you about
your grandparents. Learn what year
they were born and what the world
was like when they were growing up.
Better yet ask your grandparents to
tell you their story!

author: Lehman Riley

Meet the Author, Lehman Riley

When I was in 3rd grade, I used to daydream about summer trips to my grandparents' house. My grandfather, Papa Lemon, fascinated me; in my eyes, he was a celebrity. I wrote my daydreams about him into this book.

I now reside in Minneapolis, Minnesota with my wife Tracy and my four children, DuVale, Nareece, Andrea and Tianna.

Meet the Illustrator, Joshua Wallace

My interest in drawing started when I could pick up a crayon and scribble. Childrens books were my first big inspiration. They taught me to never neglect the depths of imagination and to never forget how to think like a child.

I currently work as an illustrator and graphic designer and live in Blaine, Minnesota.

The Adventures of Papa Lemon's Little Wanderers

Other Papa Lemon Adventures:

Book 1: Meeting Dr. Martin Luther King
Book 2: The Dangerous Escape from Slavery
Book 3: World War II, The Navajo Wind Talkers
Book 4: The Life of Babe Didrikson "Greatness is Never Forgotten"

Look for More Adventures with Papa Lemon
Visit www.papalemonedu.com to order